A JIGSAW JONES MYSTERY

The Case from Outer Space

A JIGSAW JONES MYSTERY

The Case from Outer Space

by James Preller

illustrated by R. W. Alley

FEIWEL AND FRIENDS

New York

A Feiwel and Friends Book

An imprint of Macmillan Publishing Group, LLC

175 Fifth Avenue, New York, NY 10010

Our books may be purchased in bulk for promotional, educational, or business
use. Please contact your local bookseller or the Macmillan Corporate and
Premium Sales Department at (800) 221-7945 ext. 5442 or by e-mail at
MacmillanSpecialMarkets@macmillan.com.

Library of Congress Cataloging-in-Publication Data is available.

ISBN 978-1-250-11018-3 (hardcover)

1 3 5 7 9 10 8 6 4 2

ISBN 978-1-250-11017-6 (paperback)

1 3 5 7 9 10 8 6 4 2

ISBN 978-1-250-11016-9 (ebook)

Book design by Véronique Lefèvre Sweet

Feiwel and Friends logo designed by Filomena Tuosto

First Edition—2017

mackids.com

This book is dedicated to three fierce women in publishing who helped bring Jigsaw Jones back to life: Rosemary Stimola, Liz Szabla, and Jean Feiwel.

CONTENTS

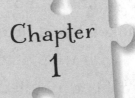

A Knock on the Door

Call me Jones.

Jigsaw Jones, private eye.

I solve mysteries. For a dollar a day, I make problems go away. I've found stolen bicycles, lost jewelry, and missing parakeets. I've even tangled with dancing ghosts and haunted scarecrows.

Mysteries can happen anywhere, at any time. One thing I've learned in this business is that anyone is a suspect. That includes friends, family, and a little green man from outer space.

Go figure.

It was a lazy Sunday morning. Outside my window, it looked like a nice spring day. The sky was blue with wispy clouds that looked like they had been painted by an artist. A swell day for a ball game. Or a mystery. Maybe both if I got lucky.

I was standing at my dining room table, staring at a 500-piece jigsaw puzzle. It was supposed to be a picture of our solar system. The sun and eight planets. But right now it was a mess. Scattered pieces lay everywhere. I scratched my head and munched on a blueberry Pop-Tart. Not too hot, not too cold. *Just right.* As a cook, I'm pretty good with a toaster. I began working on the border, grouping all the pieces that had a flat edge. Sooner or later, I'd work my way through the planets. The rust red of Mars. The rings of Saturn. And the green tint of Neptune. I've never met a puzzle I couldn't

solve. That's because I know the secret. The simple trick? Don't give up.

Don't ever give up.

My dog, Rags, leaped at the door. He barked and barked. A minute later, the doorbell rang. *Ding-a-ling, ding-dong.* That's the thing about Rags. He's faster than a doorbell. People have been coming to our house all his life. But for my dog, it's always the most exciting thing that ever happened.

Every single time.

"Get the door, Worm," my brother Billy said. He was sprawled on the couch, reading a book. Teenagers, yeesh.

"Why me?" I complained.

"Because I'm not doing it."

Billy kept reading.

Rags kept barking.

And the doorbell kept ringing.

Somebody was in a hurry.

I opened the door. Joey Pignattano and Danika Starling were standing on my stoop.

We were in the same class together, room 201, with Ms. Gleason.

"Hey, Jigsaw!" Danika waved. She bounced on her toes. The bright beads in her hair clicked and clacked.

"Boy, am I glad to see you!" Joey exclaimed. He burst into the room. "Got any water?"

"I would invite you inside, Joey," I said, "but you beat me to it."

Danika smiled.

"I ate half a bag of Jolly Ranchers this morning," Joey announced. "Now my tongue feels super weird!"

"That's not good for your teeth," I said.

Joey looked worried. "My tongue isn't good for my teeth? Are you sure? They both live inside my mouth."

"Never mind," I said.

"Pipe down, guys!" Billy complained. "I'm reading here."

"Come into the kitchen," I told Joey and Danika. "We'll get fewer complaints. Besides, I've got grape juice. It's on the house."

"On the house?" Joey asked. "Is it safe?"

I blinked. "What?"

"You keep grape juice on your roof?" Joey asked.

Danika gave Joey a friendly shove. "Jigsaw said 'on the house.' He means it's free, Joey," she said, laughing.

Joey pushed back his glasses with an index finger. "Free? In that case, I'll take a big glass."

Chapter 2

One Small Problem

I poured three glasses of grape juice.

"Got any snacks?" Joey asked. "Cookies? Chips? Corn dogs? Crackers?"

"Corn dogs?" I repeated. "Seriously?"

"Oh, they are delicious," Joey said. "I ate six yesterday. Or was that last week? I forget."

Danika shook her head and giggled. Joey always made her laugh.

I set out a bowl of chips.

Joey pounced like a football player on a

fumble. He was a skinny guy, but he ate like a rhinoceros.

"So what's up?" I asked.

"We found a note," Danika began.

"Aliens are coming," Joey interrupted. He chomped on a fistful of potato chips.

I waited for Joey to stop chewing. It took a while. *Hum-dee-dum, dee-dum-dum.* I finally asked, "What do you mean, aliens?"

"Aliens, Jigsaw!" he exclaimed. "Little green men from Mars—from the stars—from outer space!"

I looked at Danika. She shrugged, palms up. "Maybe," she said. "You never know."

I took a long swig of grape juice. "You mentioned a note," I said to Danika.

She sat tall, eyes wide. "It's very mysterious, Jigsaw. That's why we came to you."

"Narffle-snarffle," Joey mumbled, his mouth still full of chips.

I leaned back in my chair. I shoved my hands into my pockets. They were empty. Business had been slow. I was a detective without a case. "Let me make a phone call," I said.

I never work alone. My partner's name is Mila Yeh. We split the money down the middle, fifty-fifty. Mila has long black hair. She's crazy about books. And she's my best friend on the planet. Together, we make a good team.

I asked Mila to meet us in my tree house. She said she'd be over in five minutes.

It took her three and a half.

Mila lived next door. And she was as quick as a rabbit.

As usual, Mila was singing. I knew the tune, but the words were different:

> *"Twinkle, twinkle, little mystery!*
> *How I wonder what you are!*
> *Could you really be up there?*
> *Do Martians wear . . . underwear?"*

"You're funny," Danika said. She beamed a warm smile in Mila's direction.

Grinning, Mila sat down, crisscross applesauce. We gathered in a snug circle. There was no choice. My tree house wasn't exactly a palace. I am not complaining. But I don't go up there on windy days. Mila's eyes were active and alert. They moved from Joey to Danika, before settling on me. "Aliens, huh?" Mila asked.

"From outer space," Joey said.

"Uh-huh," Mila replied. If she thought Joey was crazy, Mila was too nice to say it out loud.

I took out my detective notebook. I opened to a clean page. With a blue pen, I wrote:

THE CASE FROM OUTER SPACE
CLIENTS: Joey and Danika
CLUES:

I left the last part blank. I didn't have any clues. I wasn't even sure I had a case. But it was better than nothing.

"Maybe we could start from the beginning," Mila suggested.

"Hold on." I slid forward an empty coin jar. "We get a dollar a day."

Joey and Danika exchanged glances. "We have one teensy-weensy problem," Danika said.

Uh-oh.

"No money," Joey confessed.

"We're flat broke," Danika said.

"That's the worst kind of broke," I sighed.

"Maybe we could trade?" Joey offered. He reached into his back pocket. His hand came out holding a hunk of smelly orange glop. "I've got some cheese!"

Mila leaned away. "You keep random cheese in your back pocket?"

"My front pockets were full," Joey explained.

I was afraid to ask. We were all afraid. No one wanted to know what was in Joey's front pockets. A frog? A hard-boiled egg? Last week's bologna sandwich? Anything was possible.

There was still the problem of payment. I did not liking working for free. It was bad for business. But I needed a mystery the way a fish needs to swim . . . the way a bird needs to fly . . . the way a three-toed South American tree sloth needs to hang upside down.

"Okay," I decided. "We'll look into it. No promises."

"Thanks, Jigsaw," Danika said.

"You can still have my cheese," Joey said. He held out the orange glop as if it were a pirate's treasure.

Mila coughed. "That's nice of you, Joey. Just hold on to it for now. For safekeeping." She turned to Danika. "Let's see that note."

Chapter 3

The First Clue

Danika pulled a white paper from her shirt pocket. With long thin fingers, she smoothed it out on the tree house floor.

The paper wasn't a full-size page. It was about the size of a cell phone. It had been folded once.

This is what it said:

STARMANN
visit
Life on Mars!
Space Invaders!
E.T.!

There was a doodle in the corner, penned in green marker. It was a drawing of an alien. The creature had a narrow chin, huge eyes, and antennae growing out of its head.

"Anybody you know?" I asked Joey.

Joey thought about it. "Nope."

Mila picked up the note. She carefully held it by the edges. "It's an index card." Mila handed the card to me.

I flipped it over. The reverse side had one red line and ten blue lines. For some

reason, the person who wrote the note used the blank side. I noticed a faint smudge of orange dust. I pointed to a shoe box behind Joey. "Hand me that box, Joey. I keep my detective supplies in there."

I pushed aside my fake mustache and decoder ring. "Ah, here we are." I pulled out a magnifying glass and a plastic baggie. "You mind if we keep the note?" I asked. "It's an important clue."

"Yeah, that's fine." Danika had the habit of touching the beads in her hair. She squeezed the bottom beads, as if to make sure they were still there. The beads weren't going anywhere.

I zipped the baggie closed.

"Where did you find it?" I asked.

"Inside a book," Joey said. "We got it at the Little Free Library on Danika's street."

"The Little Free Who?" I said.

"Library," Joey repeated.

I took off my baseball cap. I scratched my head. "That's what I thought you said. But what in the world is a Little Free Library?"

"It's a library," Danika explained. "But not really." She paused, thinking. "Kind of."

"Sort of," Joey added helpfully. "A little one. Except you get to keep the books forever."

My mouth opened, but no words came out.

Unfortunately, a bug flew in. *Ptooey!* I hate when that happens. I don't mind catching flies—as long as I'm playing baseball. But I'm not a fan of eating bugs. Yuck. I don't know how frogs do it.

Mila placed a hand on my arm. "Maybe if they showed us," she suggested.

"Good idea," I said.

I scribbled a few words in my detective journal. At the bottom I wrote:

ORANGE DUST????

Something told me it was an important clue. We'd need to take a closer look at that dust later.

Joey was the first to climb down the ladder. A foot from the ground, he leaped and cried, "Look out below!" Danika followed.

"Hey," Mila called down. "We forgot to ask. What was the name of the book with the note?"

Joey swallowed. He glanced at Danika. "That's the thing," he said.

"What's the thing?" I asked.

"*Messages from Mars*," Danika said. "The book was titled *Messages from Mars*."

Chapter 4

The Little Free Library

We walked a few blocks to Danika's street. After a long winter, it was nice to hear birds in the trees. A few yellow flowers poked their heads out of the ground. The grass looked greener than it did yesterday. I carried a small drawstring backpack filled with two books. Danika said I might need them, but they had to be books that I was willing to give away. I grabbed an old Nate the Great and a Ballpark Mystery from my shelves. Great books, but I wasn't going to read them again.

Danika explained the Little Free Library. "It just appeared last week, right there on the Pulvers' lawn."

She described it as a wooden box on a pole. It had a glass window and two shelves, and it was filled with books.

"How many books?" I asked.

Danika shrugged. "Ten, twenty, maybe. You'll see. There's a sign that says, 'Take a Book, Leave a Book.'"

"And that's it?" I asked. "Who's in charge?"

"Nobody," Joey said.

"My mom says that it's the honor system," Danika explained. "Take a book, leave a book. That's the only rule."

"I've heard about these Little Libraries," Mila said. "It's a thing now."

"It's a thing?" I said.

"Yeah, you know," she replied.

I didn't know, but I kept my trap shut. I had already swallowed enough flies for today.

There was an old man at the Little Library when we arrived. He wore baggy pants and a red-checked jacket. A brown turban was wrapped around his head.

"Hey, Mr. Kaleel. Find anything you like?" Danika asked.

The old man turned slowly, shuffling his big feet. His back was slightly hunched. He smiled at us. "I like to check what they've got. The books change every few days."

"What do you like to read?" Danika asked.

"This and that," the old man said dreamily. "Whatever catches my fancy."

He walked away, slow-footed and empty-handed.

"He lives across the street," Danika told us.

The library was painted orange and blue—the colors of my favorite baseball team, the New York Mets. I liked it already.

The library had books for adults and children. Good ones, too.

"Hmmm," Mila said. She ran her fingers down her long black hair, lost in thought.

"Hmmm?" I repeated. "Was that a good 'Hmmm' or a bad 'Hmmm'?"

"Maybe it's nothing," she said. "But there are a lot of books about planets and space travel in here."

The house in the yard was painted blue with white trim. A redbrick walkway led up to the front door. I needed answers. I knew I'd be leaning on that doorbell in a minute. First, I wanted a closer look at these books.

"We should go through each one," I said.

I handed a short stack to Joey. His eyes widened. "You want me to read them all?"

"No, Joey. Just flip through the pages. See if you find anything unusual."

A few minutes later, Mila said, "Bingo!" She had found another piece of paper. It was the same size as the other clue.

Mila held it out for us to see.

LET
TOM
PICK
ON
MAY

Danika read the message aloud. "'LET TOM PICK ON MAY.' That's weird. What does it mean?"

I looked at Mila. "It might be a secret code."

"Perhaps," Mila said. "Maybe it means exactly what it says. Some guy named Tom is picking on May."

We didn't know anyone by either name.

"I'm hungry," Joey complained.

"Not now, Joey. We're hunting for clues." I compared this note to the first one. "Same handwriting," I noted. "The writer makes little circles to dot the letter *i*."

"It's neat," Mila observed. "Printed. Not cursive."

I looked at the cover of the book where Mila had found the note. It was an old copy of *Mr. Popper's Penguins*.

"I love that book," Danika said. "We read it in school."

"See what I mean, Jigsaw," Joey said. He pressed close to me. "Definitely aliens."

I wasn't so sure about that. But he was right about one thing. There was something fishy going on. *Glub, glub, glub.* While Mila, Joey, and Danika kept looking for clues, I did push-ups on the Pulvers' doorbell. A smiling woman with short hair answered the door.

I told her that I was a detective.

"How thrilling," she said.

"I am working on a case," I explained. "Do you mind if I ask you a few questions?"

I showed her my card:

NEED A MYSTERY SOLVED?

Call **Jigsaw Jones** or **Mila Yeh**, **Private Eyes!**

Mrs. Pulver whistled. "Wowee zowee."

"It's a living," I said.

She told me about the library. She said that she read about Little Free Libraries on the Internet. "I thought it was a wonderful idea," she said. "So I asked Harold to build one."

I raised an eyebrow. "Harold?"

"My husband," she replied. "He's retired. I like to give him little jobs."

I asked, "Have you noticed anything . . . strange?"

"Oh, Harold has been strange for years," she said, laughing.

"No, I mean about the library," I said.

She clasped her hands. "Lots of folks come and go. Friends, neighbors, even people I've never seen before. It's lovely, actually. The books connect us."

I thanked her and said good-bye.

"Toodle-oo!" she said. "Remember: Take a book, leave a book."

Which was exactly what I did.

Twice.

Chapter 5

Room 201

I don't love Monday mornings. They come too soon. I yawned and waited for the school bus. Mila swiped a finger across her nose. It was our secret signal. She tucked a paper into my palm.

I glanced at the note:

4-15 25-15-21 18-5-1-12-12-25

2-5-12-9-5-22-5 9-14 19-16-1-3-5

1-12-9-5-14-19?

It was in code. Not a problem. This was an easy one. Mila must have been in a hurry. It's called a Substitution Code. Each number stands for a letter in the alphabet. Number 1 is letter *A*. Number 2 is letter *B*. Number 3 is letter *C*. All the way to 26 for letter *Z*.

On the bus, I wrote two columns with the numbers and letters in my notebook. Figuring out the message was easy after that. Anybody can do it.

"Well? What's your answer to my question?" Mila asked.

I pulled down my cap. "I'm a detective. It doesn't matter what I believe. My job is to follow the clues. I believe in facts."

Behind us, I heard Joey talking to Ralphie Jordan and Geetha Nair. He bragged, "I am helping Jigsaw. We're searching for aliens from outer space."

Mila looked at me. She raised an eyebrow.

"That sounds fun," Ralphie said.

"I'm Jigsaw's right-hand man," Joey said. "Even though I'm a lefty."

Kim Lewis joined the conversation. Kim had short hair and three freckles on the tip of her nose. "Bobby Solofsky once saw a flying saucer," she said.

I glanced back. Geetha gulped. She looked pale and worried.

"I doubt it," Ralphie said. "Bobby is always making up stories."

"I believe it," Joey said. "It's called a UFO. An . . . Under . . . Flying . . . Something."

Mila turned around. She explained, "UFO means an Unidentified Flying Object."

"Whatever!" Ralphie laughed.

We hurried to room 201. We loved our teacher, Ms. Gleason. She was better than a cold glass of lemonade on a summer day. "Good morning, boys and girls. I hope you all had a nice weekend."

"It was too short," Bigs Maloney grumbled.

"Weekends should last all week!" Lucy Hiller agreed. Everyone liked that idea, even Ms. Gleason.

After morning announcements, Ms. Gleason got us moving. She often says, "We have to wake up our bodies and our

The
earth
turns
around!

brains!" We did exercises, sang songs, and danced. Today, she taught us a new song. It sounded like "The Farmer in the Dell" but a lot worse.

The earth turns around,
The earth turns around,

Once a day, every day,
The earth turns around.

The moon goes round the earth,
The moon goes round the earth,
Once a month, every month,
The moon goes round the earth.

The earth goes round the sun,
The earth goes round the sun,
Once a year, every year,
The earth goes round the sun.

We added dance steps. Lucy was great at that. We twirled in circles. But that didn't last long. Stringbean Noonan said his stomach felt dizzy. His face turned greenish. That made Ms. Gleason nervous. So we all sat down.

"I am so excited for this week," Ms. Gleason told us. "We will be having a surprise visitor from far, far away!"

Everybody started asking questions at once.

Ms. Gleason raised her hand. "No, no, no," she said. "I can't tell you. Otherwise it wouldn't be a surprise."

"Rats," Helen Zuckerman muttered.

"Snails," Bobby Solofsky groaned.

"Cookies," Joey said.

"Cookies?" Mila asked.

Joey's eyes brightened. "Do you have any?"

"No," Mila said. "You said *cookies*. I wondered why."

Joey touched his belly. "A guy can dream, can't he?"

Our Solar System

We gathered around the reading rug. "As you know, I love science," Ms. Gleason said. "We don't do much science in second grade. But this week, we will explore . . . our solar system! We will do art projects, watch videos, read books, and—"

"Sing songs!" Kim said.

"That's right, Kim," Ms. Gleason. "All week long we are going to celebrate our neighborhood in space. Our solar system is in the Milky Way galaxy."

"Milky Way?" Joey said hopefully.

"I'm sorry, Joey. We are talking about space—not the candy bar," Ms. Gleason said.

Joey frowned. A few of us giggled.

I noticed two new posters on the wall. Both were about planets. "You've been decorating," I said.

"Thank you for noticing, Jigsaw. Good detective work." Ms. Gleason winked. "I came in on Sunday. I thought the room needed sprucing up." She pointed to a red basket. "I also organized all our space books in one place. There are new books in there, too. I've been updating our collection. Out with the old, in with the new. Be sure to check them out. Remember, space is the place!"

She opened a nonfiction book titled *The Planets*. Ms. Gleason explained that the sun is a star, not a planet. It is much, much bigger than the earth. "Imagine that the sun is the size of a basketball." Ms. Gleason picked up a marker and made a green dot

on the whiteboard. "That tiny dot would be the earth."

We learned about the eight planets: Mercury, Venus, Earth, Mars, Jupiter, Saturn, Uranus, and Neptune.

"That's a lot to remember," Bigs said.

"Here's a trick to help you remember," Ms. Gleason said. She wrote on the board:

My
Very
Educated
Mother
Just
Served
Us
Nachos

Everybody thought the same thing: *Huh?*

"Oh, I get it," Mila said. "It's the first letter for every planet. *My* equals *Mercury*. *Very* stands for *Venus!*"

"And *Nachos* stands for delicious!" Joey joked.

After she finished reading, Ms. Gleason tucked a bookmark into the book. "We'll get back to this tomorrow. I believe it's almost time for P.E."

During recess, we climbed on the pirate ship.

But we didn't play pirates. All the talk was about aliens. Half the kids said they believed in aliens. "Sure, I believe," Mike Radcliff said. "I bet flying saucers visit earth all the time."

"Why don't we ever see them?" Mila wondered.

"It's top secret," Mike replied. "The government doesn't want anyone to know. They keep it all hidden so we don't go nuts."

Bobby Solofsky stepped forward. "I saw one. I woke up in the middle of the night. There was a weird noise outside. *Bzzzz*,

bzzzz," he droned. "So I looked out my window. I saw bright, flashing lights . . ."

"Pssst. Hey, Jigsaw. Can I talk to you and Mila?" Joey yanked on my arm.

"Easy on the arm, Joey. I might need it someday," I said.

Joey looked around. He whispered, "In private."

He led us to the swing set. He sat down and waited, looking back at me. So I gave him a shove.

"Okay, Joey. What do you want?"

"I want to help you guys," he said. "I could be a detective, too. You could teach me."

I scratched the back of my neck. "I don't know, Joey. . . ."

Mila poked me with an elbow. "We could use help with the stakeout."

"The stakeout!" Joey exclaimed. "I love stakeouts! I am awesome at stakeouts!" He paused, then asked in a soft voice, "What's a stakeout?"

My knees began to itch.

A small headache formed behind my eyes.

Mila spoke to Joey. "We need to keep an eye on the Little Free Library. I have a piano lesson today. Jigsaw can't do it all by himself. Your job, Joey, is to hide and watch."

"Hide and watch," Joey repeated.

"See who comes by," Mila said.

"I can keep two eyes on it," Joey offered. He pointed at his eyeballs to make sure we understood.

I looked at Mila. I wasn't sure about this.

"It's fine, Jigsaw," she said. "Joey can help. What could go wrong?"

A lot, I thought. But I didn't say a word. Instead I said, "We need to find out who left those notes. That's the key, Joey."

"There's a key?" Joey asked.

"Never mind," I replied.

Chapter 7

The Stakeout

Joey took the first turn at the stakeout. I relaxed at home. I ate a snack. I worked on the puzzle. And I thought about Joey Pignattano. He sure was eager to work on the case. Maybe too eager. At 4:30, I decided to check on him.

I got on my bike and pedaled there.

Joey was "hiding" in a patch of bushes across the street. He was easy to find. The bushes were small, and Joey was dressed in a bright yellow jacket. When he saw me,

Joey jumped up. He waved both arms. He shouted, "Here I am, Jigsaw! Over here! On the stakeout!"

He seemed pretty happy.

"Any action?" I asked.

"Not really," Joey said. "I had a great idea

from the movie *E.T.* Did you ever see that movie, Jigsaw?"

"Sure, it's about the alien who gets stuck on earth. *Phone home*," I added, in my best E.T. voice.

Joey laughed. "That's it—my favorite movie! I left a trail of Reese's Pieces from the library to my hiding spot."

"Why?" I wondered.

"To catch the Star Man," Joey said. "From the note."

"Right," I said, nodding. "So what happened?"

"I got hungry," Joey admitted.

"Joey, you didn't."

"Yeah, I ate them all. I guess that plan didn't work so hot," he said.

That reminded me. "Joey, Mila and I discovered traces of orange dust on the note. Were you eating Doritos that morning?"

"Nope."

"Really? What about Cheetos?" I asked.

"I don't like those, either," Joey said. "I prefer my cheese in slices, hunks, or liquid form."

"You're sure about that?" I asked.

"That orange dust didn't come from me," Joey said. "I had cereal and Jolly Ranchers for breakfast that morning."

Hmmm, I thought. It all came back to the note. That was the key to the mystery. "So nobody came by?" I asked.

"Oh, I almost forgot," Joey said. "Ms. Gleason stopped at the Little Free Library."

That surprised me. Then I thought about it. School was only three blocks away. Ms. Gleason probably drove past on her way to work.

"She traded in three old books and took three new ones," Joey added.

"Really? Did you see which ones?" I asked.

Joey shook his head. "I was hiding, like you told me."

"Good," I replied. "Are you sure she didn't see you?"

Joey paused. His mouth said "No," but his head nodded yes.

He had me confused.

I repeated the question as if I were talking to my dog. "Did . . . she . . . see . . . you?"

Joey shrugged. His nose twitched. "Maybe, sort of."

"Maybe," I echoed.

"Well, she waved to me," Joey admitted.

I took off my baseball cap and scratched my head. Talking to Joey always made me itchy.

He continued, "She asked me why I was sitting in the bushes." Joey looked upset. "Did I do bad?"

Poor guy. He tried his best. I sighed and said, "No, Joey. You did great. You did really, really great. This is a big help." I patted him on the back.

Joey smiled pure sunbeams. Proud as a peacock.

"Thanks, Jigsaw!"

He seemed three inches taller.

Joey went home. I climbed a tree. Nothing happened. No one else stopped at the Little Free Library.

Up in the tree, I thought about the case. And the books. And Ms. Gleason. Our teacher had become the key to the mystery.

Chapter 8

A Little Help from My Friends

That night, I sat alone at the dining room table. The puzzle was started. But my mind drifted to the case. I took out the two notes. I stared at them under a magnifying glass.

What did the words mean?

Who wrote them?

I reached for the second index card.

LET
TOM
PiCK
ON
MAY

Let Tom pick on May. It might have been a code. I couldn't crack it. I wondered if it was a First Letter Scramble. I tried making new words out of the first letters. PLOMT! MOPLT! TPOML!

No luck. I pushed the card aside.

I turned to the first note.

STARMANN
visit
Life on Mars!
Space Invaders!
E.T.!

I drew a line between STAR and MANN. *Star mann visit.* It bothered me that *man* was spelled wrong. The other words were spelled correctly. It seemed like a strange mistake for such an easy word.

I felt sure both notes were written by the same person. The letters were similar. The green ink, too. I examined the orange dust. I tasted it. Yes, it was cheesy. I wondered if it was true about Joey. Did he really not like Cheetos? Could Joey be lying? *Was it possible there was a food that Joey* didn't *like?*

And then I wondered: *Why would Joey lie?*

A voice interrupted my thoughts. "Earth to Jigsaw. Come in, Jigsaw."

"Huh?" My head turned. My grandmother sat down across from me.

"What have you got there? Homework?" she asked.

"I'm working on a case." I told Grams all about it.

"Very interesting," Grams said. "If you ask me, it's possible. Maybe one day aliens will visit earth. I doubt we're alone in the universe."

"Really?"

Grams took off her glasses. She rubbed her eyelids with the tips of her fingers. Her hair was thin and white. But her mind was sharp. "Of course," she said. "The universe is huge. It contains billions of stars. Millions of planets. Why should we be the only ones?"

"But we don't know for sure," I said.

"No," Grams said, smiling. "The answer is . . . we don't know the answer! Isn't that wonderful? Don't you love it?"

"I'd rather know," I said.

Grams replied, "Oh well, that's the way the cookie crumbles. I am old enough to remember the day astronauts first landed on the moon. *Apollo 11*. It was in the summer of 1969. Long before you were born. We watched on a blurry, black-and-white television set. Those men were so brave. I'll never forget that day for as long as I live." She looked at me, eyes gleaming. "We walked on the moon. Imagine that!"

Grams looked away, remembering. Old people are filled with memories, like a glass filled to the top with grape juice. I guess I'm lucky. I have three brothers and a sister. And that's fine, most of the time. But I've also got Grams. That's great every day of the week.

My brother Billy paused next to me. He studied the puzzle pieces.

"Jigsaw is studying clues," Grams informed him. She gestured to the notes.

Billy pointed to the second note. "Just the way I like my sandwiches."

"What do you mean?" I asked.

Billy read: "Lettuce, Tomato, Pickle, Onion, Mayo."

My jaw dropped open. "They are abbreviations! Of course! A grocery list!" I exclaimed. "Billy, you're brilliant!"

"Yeah, I've been waiting for someone to notice," he said, grinning. Then, as easy as one, two, three, he popped three puzzle pieces into place.

I hate when people do that.

I got up to call Mila. She answered on the second ring. I explained about the note. "Billy figured it out," I said.

"Great work, partner," she said.

"Not so fast," I replied. "Joey saw something. It might be important. Ms. Gleason took three books from the Little Free Library. I wish I knew which ones."

"I can check the list," Mila said.

"That's the problem," I said. "I didn't make a list."

Mila laughed. "We're a team, Jigsaw. While you talked to Mrs. Pulver, I wrote down the title of every book in the library."

"You're amazing," I said. "Now we'll know without asking Ms. Gleason. I don't think she'd like it if we were spying. We should keep that on the down low."

"I'll stop by the library on the way to school," Mila said. "We're getting closer, Jigsaw."

"Yes," I said. "Thanks to a little help from my friends."

Mila was silent.

"What are you thinking?" I asked.

"We need proof," Mila said. "I don't want to be wrong about Ms. Gleason."

She was right. But that's Mila. She's usually right.

For the next two days, we worked the case.

Chapter 9

Working the Case

It was a busy few days in room 201. We made mini books about planets. We did art projects. And every day, we watched videos about astronauts and space travel.

Helen Zuckerman made a poster that compared the size of the planets with fruit. Mars was a blueberry, Earth was a strawberry, Saturn was a grapefruit, and Jupiter—the biggest planet—was a watermelon!

I didn't think aliens were coming.

But something was definitely up.

On Wednesday morning, Mila and Danika searched the red basket of space books. They found three books from the list. Three books that Ms. Gleason got from the Little Free Library.

Strike one.

I lifted a piece of paper out of the garbage. It had Ms. Gleason's handwriting on it. That night, I compared it to the notes. They matched. The same ink. The same shape to the letters.

Strike two.

After music, Mila was the first one back to class. She saw Ms. Gleason reading a book. "Hi," Mila said.

Ms. Gleason smiled. She tucked an index card into her book. And closed it. "Do you need anything?" Ms. Gleason asked.

"Nada," Mila said. She had already gotten what she needed: more proof. Ms. Gleason used random pieces of paper as bookmarks.

Strike three.

Danika learned that Ms. Gleason loves Doritos. That fact linked her to the orange dust. It wasn't proof, but our case was coming together.

It was time to act.

Mila, Joey, Danika, and I stayed after class to have a little talk with our teacher.

"Tell me, Ms. Gleason," I said. "What do you think about . . . MAYONNAISE?"

"Excuse me?"

"Some people like eating it," I said. "What about you?"

"I, um . . ." She blinked a few times. "It's fine. I like it."

"Aha!" I said. I made a note in my detective journal:

LIKES MAYO.

"How about pickles? Do they tickle your fancy?" I asked.

"Jigsaw, what's this all about?" she asked.

I placed the palms of my hands on her desk. I leaned in. "I'm working a case. You might be the key."

"Oh dear." Ms. Gleason brought a hand to her mouth. "This sounds serious."

Mila pushed forward. She handed the first note to Ms. Gleason. "Does that look familiar?"

"Oh, yes," she said. "Where did you find this?"

"In a book," Joey said.

Danika nodded. "Yeah, a book."

"We want to know what's going on," I said. "Who is Starmann? Why did you draw that picture?"

"Yeah," Joey said. "And are little green aliens coming to take over the planet?"

We all stopped to look at Joey.

"Sorry." He shrugged. "I got excited."

Ms. Gleason smiled. "I can't fool you guys. It's about our special visitor tomorrow. From far, far away."

"May I ask who?" I said.

"You may ask, but I'm not telling. You'll have to wait until tomorrow," Ms. Gleason said.

We heard a man's voice down the hall. "Last call for buses. Everybody out!"

"Yikes!" Danika cried. We raced out of there lickety-split.

Chapter 10

A Surprise Visit

On Friday afternoon, everyone from grades 1 to 3 squished into the library. We buzzed with excitement. We faced the screen. Our librarian, Mrs. Ventura, tapped on the computer. Suddenly, a smiling face appeared on the screen.

A gasp filled the room.

We were meeting a real live astronaut.

"Hello, boys and girls!" the astronaut said.

I heard Lucy whisper, "Major Starmann is a woman."

"And she looks like my mom," Danika said.

"Greetings, Major Starmann. We are so excited," Ms. Gleason gushed. "Thank you for taking time out to Skype with our students. Most of us have never met an astronaut before. I know I'm thrilled. We have so many questions."

"It's my pleasure," Major Starmann said. "I love meeting young students."

The visit flew by. Major Doreen Starmann had been an astronaut for fifteen years. She told us about floating in space—she called it "zero gravity"—and about her time living in the space station.

Toward the end, Stringbean asked, "How do you take baths in space?"

"There are no showers or bathtubs," Major Starmann explained. "In the morning, we squeeze a few drops of water from a tube into a towel. That's how we wash off."

A third grader asked about going to the bathroom.

"I knew somebody would ask that!" Major

Starmann laughed. And with a wink she said, "Bathrooms are private—just like on earth. Next question?"

"How do you sleep in space?" someone asked.

Major Starmann said that all astronauts have their own rooms, called crew quarters.

They're the size of a small closet. "I keep photos of my family in there. Personal things. It's too small for a bed. Remember, there's no gravity. We don't have to lie down. We sleep in sleeping bags tied to the wall."

"Oh my, I don't know if I could get used to

that," Ms. Gleason said. She glanced at the wall clock. "We are almost out of time. Who has a final question?"

I wanted to ask about aliens. I wanted to ask, *Is there life in outer space?* But I felt shy and embarrassed. It was easier to stay silent.

Ms. Gleason nodded at Mila. "Is it hard to become an astronaut?" Mila wondered.

"Oh yes," Major Starmann said, laughing. "I am very lucky to have this wonderful job. But I also worked very, very hard in school. That's my advice—especially for you girls out there. The world needs more women scientists. Study hard. Dream big. Reach for the stars. Who knows, you just might get there!"

Walking back to class, Mila and I caught up with Joey. "That was awesome!" he exclaimed.

Mila agreed. "*Reach for the stars.* I liked that."

"*Dream big*," Joey said. "Just like I dreamed about becoming a detective. It came true."

I put a hand on Joey's shoulder. "Well, that closes the case. Too bad. No little green men from Mars."

"I owe you guys," Joey said. He started to reach into his pocket. I didn't want to see what he might pull out.

"No charge," I quickly said. "Besides, we couldn't have solved it without your help."

"For real?" Joey asked.

"Absolutely," I said.

"Are you sure you don't want any cheese?" Joey offered.

"Totally!" Mila and I said at once.

We laughed all the way back to room 201.

The Stars Above

It was Friday night. My mother was out with friends. My father sat in a chair, staring at his laptop. The case was closed. My puzzle was finished. There was nothing to do. I lay on the carpet with Rags. And sighed.

My father snapped the computer shut. "What's the matter, Jigsaw? You seem blue."

"I don't know. I guess I never really solved the mystery," I said.

He didn't understand.

"Up there." I pointed to the ceiling. "In space. Are we alone?"

He thought for a moment, tapping a finger against his lips. "Give me five minutes," he said. "Do me a favor, Jigsaw. See if Grams wants to come for a ride?"

"Where are we going?" I asked.

"To look for little green creatures from outer space," he said.

"But it's almost bedtime."

"Up to you," he replied.

Fifteen minutes later, Grams, my father, and I walked out behind the high school. It was dark. I held the flashlight. My father walked behind me, with Grams at his elbow. "Watch your step, Mom," he said.

"We're here," he announced.

I looked around. The flashlight beam sliced through the darkness.

"Turn it off, Jigsaw," he said.

The world went black.

It was as dark as a closet.

"So?" I asked.

"Look up," Grams said.

The night sky was thick with stars. They seemed closer than ever before.

"If you want to go stargazing, you have to get away from the lights," my father said.

"It reminds me of a famous poem by Walt

Whitman," Grams said. "When he gazes in perfect silence at the stars."

My father reached into his jacket pocket. He pulled out two small cans, attached by a string. "Let's try an experiment," he said.

He told me to hold a can to my ear.

"Listen very carefully," he said. "Maybe we'll hear aliens."

He held the other can up to the sky.

"Well, any news?" Grams asked.

"Of course not," I said. "It's just string and a tin can. How am I going to hear aliens with this?"

"That's the point, Jigsaw. Every year, scientists learn more. They watch the stars with powerful telescopes. They listen for signals. And every year, our machines improve," my father said. "If there's life up there, someday we might hear it. But first we might need to invent a really good telephone!"

"*Phone home*," I said in my scratchy E.T. voice.

My father pointed a crooked finger to the sky. "*Home*," he said.

We both laughed.

"Oh, hush, you two," Grams said. "Just look at the stars."

And so we did.

We stood in an open field.

In the dark of night.

And gazed at the stars.

In perfect silence.

"That's the real mystery, Jigsaw," my father said. "Are we alone in the universe? We don't know yet. It's a mystery that can't be solved—even by the best detectives."

"Not yet," I said, gazing into the night sky. "Not yet."

After a while, we headed to the car.

My father led the way. He took the flashlight.

I walked with Grams.
She held my elbow.
We went slowly.
"Careful," I said.
And together we headed back.
Home.

Thank you for reading this **FEIWEL AND FRIENDS** book.

The Friends who made

The Case from
Outer Space

possible are:

Jean Feiwel, Publisher

Liz Szabla, Associate Publisher

Rich Deas, Senior Creative Director

Holly West, Editor

Alexei Esikoff, Senior Managing Editor

Raymond Ernesto Colón, Senior Production Manager

Anna Roberto, Editor

Christine Barcellona, Editor

Emily Settle, Administrative Assistant

Anna Poon, Assistant Editor

Follow us on Facebook or visit us online at mackids.com.

OUR BOOKS ARE FRIENDS FOR LIFE.